Padma Shri Pran

Maurice Horn, the editor of World Encyclopedia of Comics, has described cartoonist PRAN as Walt Disney of India.

Entertaining generation after generation, his comics have been constant companion of all the growing youngsters providing fun and amusement through his famous characters like CHACHA CHAUDHARY, SABU, SHRIMATIJI, PINKI, BILLOO, RAMAN etc. More than 600 of his titles are selling well in the market, and numerous comic strips are regularly appearing in various newspapers. His CHACHA CHAUDHARY comics had already been adapted for a TV Serial, and ran continuously for 600 episodes on a premier channel.

Travelling widely over the globe, he delivers lectures at various International Conferences. He has also been honoured with 'People of The Year Award' by Limca Book of Records for popularizing comics. His comic book 'United We Stand' was released in 1983 by the then Prime Minister Mrs. Indira Gandhi, and is still very popular among children.

Publisher

OH ! IT DIDN'T GO
VERY FAR.

YOU'RE BRAGGING.
TRY THROWING THIS.

HU-HUBA !
??

SWISHHH !

THE BALL HAS FALLEN IN THAT DILAPIDATED BUILDING

IT'S HERE. IT WENT FARTHER THAN I HAD EXPECTED.

WHOSE MASK IS THIS?

APPEARS TO BE CENTURIES OLD.

LET'S TAKE THE MASK TO CHACHAJI.

YOU'VE PROVED TO BE A USELESS HUSBAND.

YOU HAVE NEVER PURCHASED A NEW DRESS OR A PIECE OF JEWELLERY. I'VE SPENT MY ENTIRE LIFE COOKING IN THE KITCHEN...

NEVER HAVE YOU TAKEN ME FOR A VACATION TO A HILL STATION. THE OTHER HUSBANDS RESPECT THEIR WIVES A LOT.

BINI ! YOU SPEAK SO MUCH, IT WILL GIVE A HEADACHE.

HEADACHE ? ME ?

NO, ME.

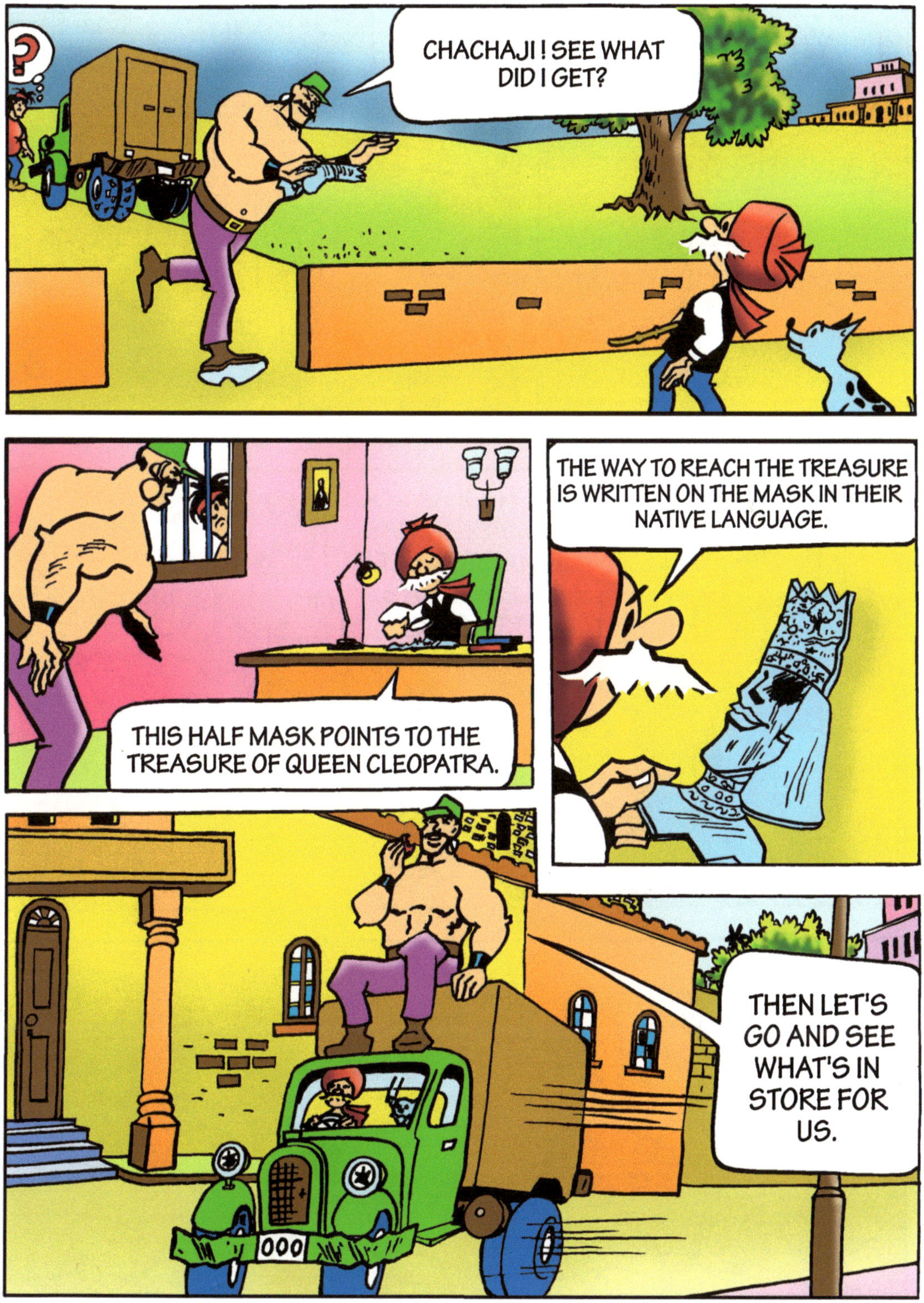

THIS HALF MASK POINTS TO THE TREASURE OF QUEEN CLEOPATRA.

THE WAY TO REACH THE TREASURE IS WRITTEN ON THE MASK IN THEIR NATIVE LANGUAGE.

THEN LET'S GO AND SEE WHAT'S IN STORE FOR US.

LET'S GO AND TELL
JUNKMAIL.

JUNKMAIL...
SHOT ! WHAT'S
THE NEWS ?

JUNK ! CHACHAJI HAS GOT
A BROKEN MASK. IT HAS
THE MAP TO QUEEN
CLEOPATRA'S
TREASURE.

SHOT ! NOW THAT
ENTIRE TREASURE
WILL BE OURS.

THERE IS JUNGLE AHEAD. WE'LL HAVE TO WALK BEYOND THIS.

ARE WE ON THE RIGHT TRACK ?

CHACHAJI ! BEWARE !

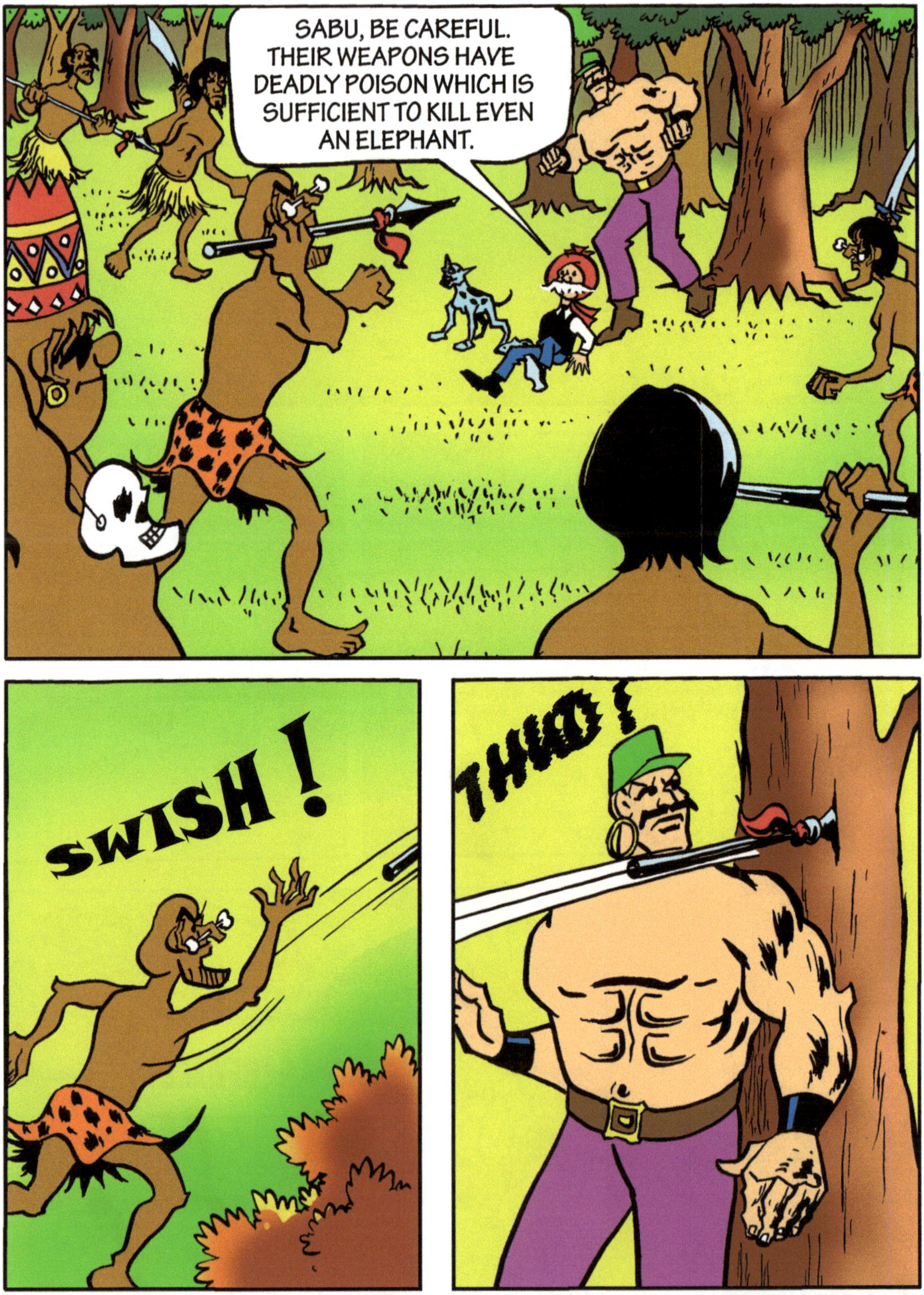

SABU, BE CAREFUL. THEIR WEAPONS HAVE DEADLY POISON WHICH IS SUFFICIENT TO KILL EVEN AN ELEPHANT.

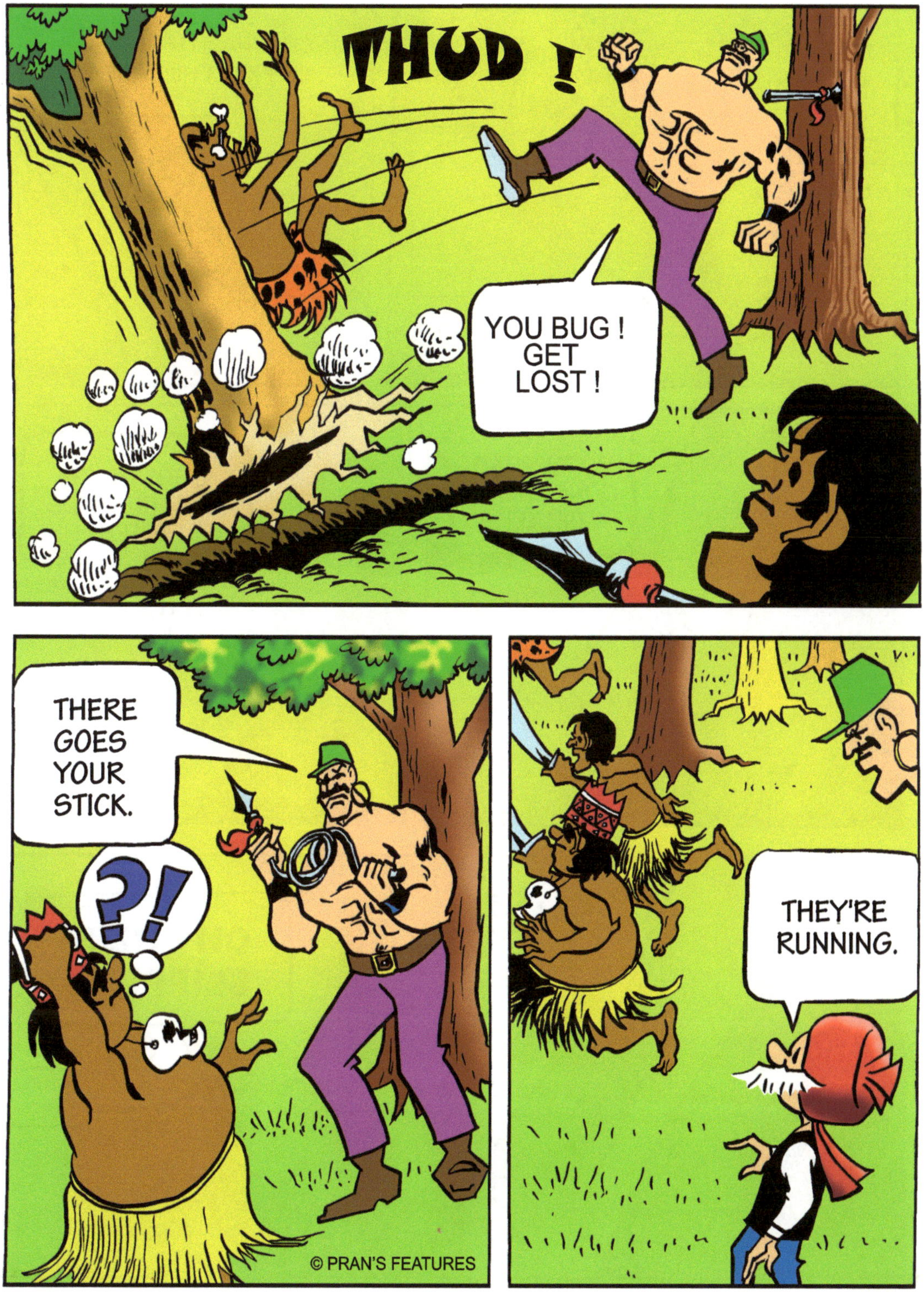

THUD !

YOU BUG ! GET LOST !

MOVE AHEAD !

CHACHAJI ! ! I CAN SEE A DIFFICULT HILL AHEAD.

ROCKET HAS GONE AHEAD OF US.

LIGHT THINGS MOVE UPWARDS FASTER.

OH ! HE'S SLIPPED !

I WAS SUCCESSFUL IN CATCHING ROCKET.

OH ! THE ROCK THAT WAS SUPPORTING ME HAS MOVED FROM ITS PLACE.

THIS CORNER HAS SAVED ME FROM FALLING.

IT'S A BEAUTIFUL SCENE HERE.

THE INSTRUCTION ON THIS MASK SAYS THAT THERE IS A HUGE OPEN GROUND AHEAD.

NEED TO BE MORE CAREFUL WHILE DESCENDING.

ROCKET SEEMS TO LIKE THE PLAINS MORE.

HERE CHACHAJI, HAVE SOME FRUITS.

ROCKET SEEMS TO LIKE THE APPLES.

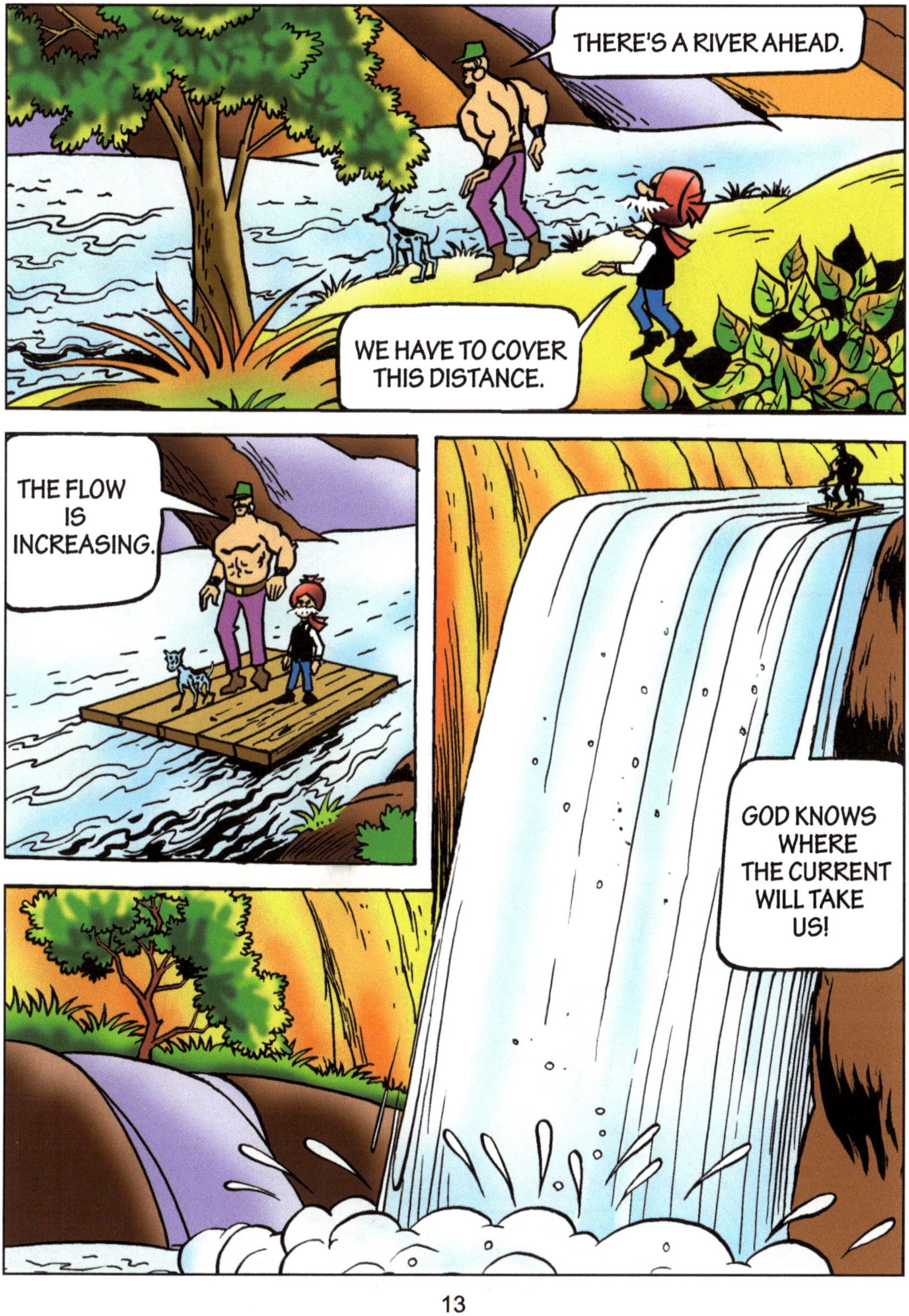

THE FLOW IS INCREASING.

GOD KNOWS WHERE THE CURRENT WILL TAKE US!

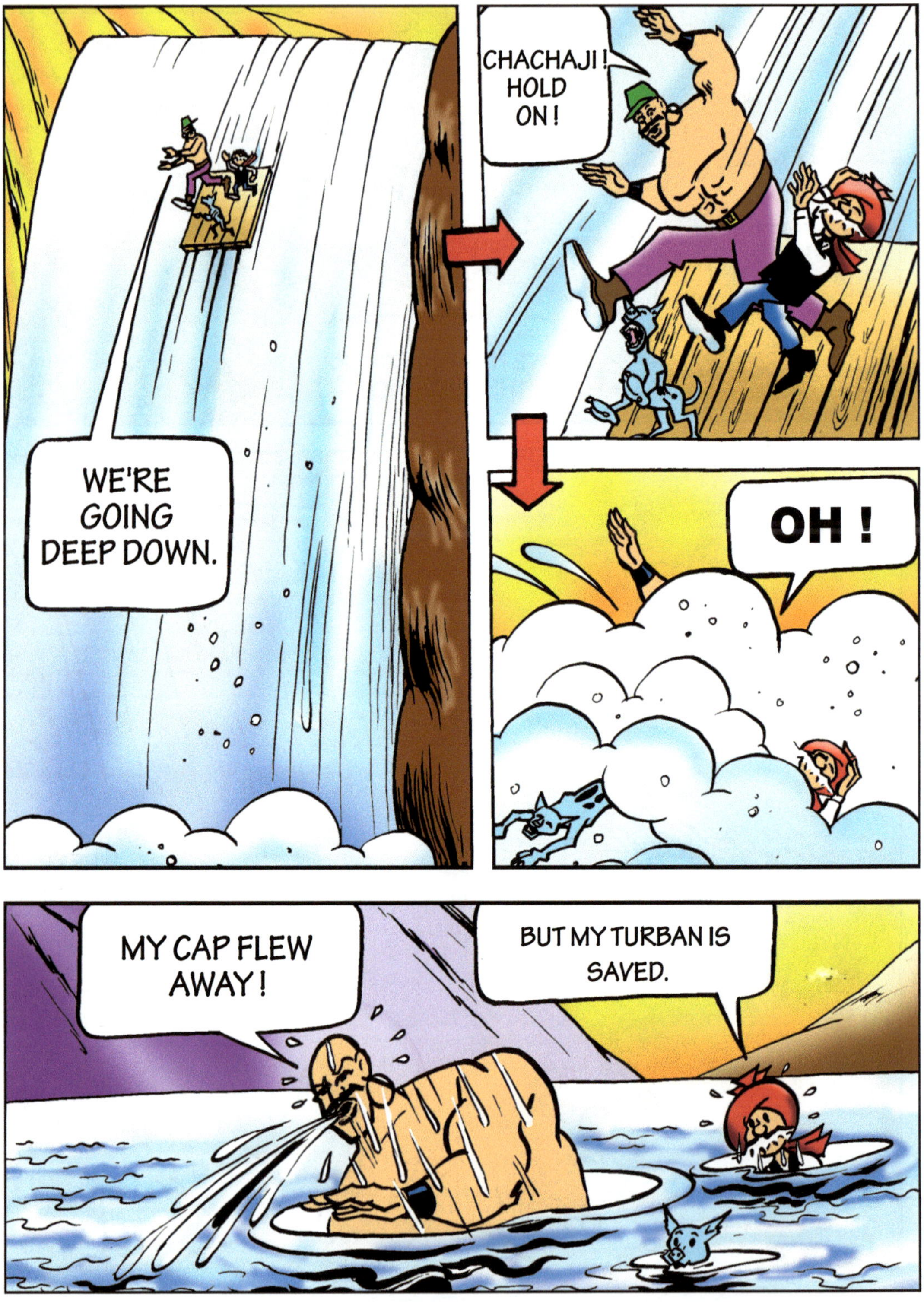

WE'RE GOING DEEP DOWN.

CHACHAJI ! HOLD ON !

OH !

GRRRR !
NEED TO STOP IT QUICKLY.
NOW IT'S A MATTER OF LIFE AND DEATH.

I AM SUCCESSFUL IN CLOSING ITS MOUTH.

OHHH ! THAT CROCODILE HAS TAKEN SABU INTO THE WATER. A CROCODILE'S POWER INCREASES IN THE WATER

IT'S TAKING ME INTO THE DEPTHS.

I SHOULD CHOKE HIM BEFORE THAT.

THE CROCODILE HAS COME UP....SABU ?

I AM VERY CURIOUS.

IT'S DEAD.
OH ! THANK HEAVENS !

CHACHAJI! WHAT ELSE DOES THIS MASK TELL?
AFTER GOING AHEAD WE'LL COME ACROSS A DOUBLE TREE. WE'VE TO GO IN THE DIRECTION IT IS BOWING.

IT'S SO PECULIAR !!
DOUBLE TREE !

THE TREE POINTS TOWARDS THE SOUTH.

CHACHAJI, YOU'VE EVEN GOT A HORSE TO RIDE.

I'LL HAVE TO JUMP IN ORDER TO RIDE ON IT.

LET'S MOVE AHEAD.

RIDING WOULD SAVE ME FROM TIREDNESS. SABU, WHAT ABOUT YOU ?
I LIKE WALKING.

YOUR JOURNEY ENDS HERE.
IF YOU WANT TO SURVIVE, THEN GIVE THE MASK TO JUNKMAIL.

OK, TAKE IT.
HO ! HO !! EVERYONE'S AFRAID OF DYING.
CHACHAJI ! NO !!

WHAT'S WRITTEN ON IT? I CAN'T READ IT.

THAT'S WHY PARENTS TELL THEIR KIDS TO STUDY WHEN THEY'RE SMALL. THE NATIVE LANGUAGE IS WRITTEN ON IT.

CHACHA CHAUDHARY'S BRAIN WORKS FASTER THAN A COMPUTER.

NO ONE WILL MOVE... ELSEI'LL SHOOT. HAND OVER THE MASK TO ME.
??

OHHH ! CHACHAJI IS IN DANGER !

OHH !
JUMPPP !
WELL DONE, ROCKET !

KILL THEM ! AND SNATCH THE MASK !
SHOOOOTTTTT !!

WHEN SABOO IS ANGRY,
A VOLCANO ERUPTS SOMEWHERE.

FROM HERE WE HAVE TO GO TO THE EAST.

ROCKET BEWARE !

HE'S FALLEN IN THE DRY WELL.
IT'S MENTIONED ON THE MASK. WE ALSO HAVE TO JUMP IN.

HU- HUBA !

THUDD D !

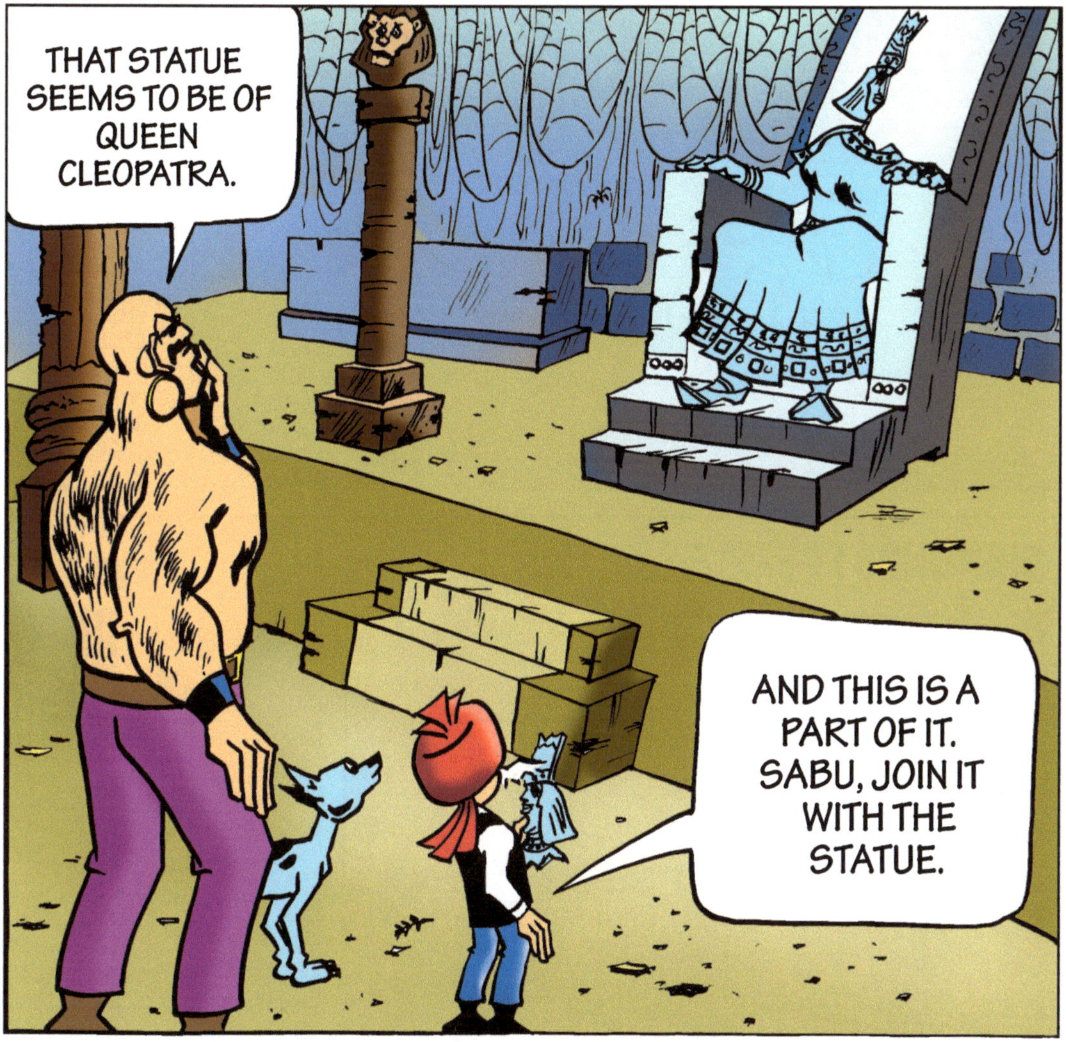

THAT STATUE SEEMS TO BE OF QUEEN CLEOPATRA.

AND THIS IS A PART OF IT. SABU, JOIN IT WITH THE STATUE.

THE DOOR OPENED IMMEDIATELY AFTER THE STATUE'S FACE WAS JOINED.
THE TREASURE SURELY IS THERE.

DIAMONDS ! PEARLS !

HU-HU-HU !

HU-HU-HU !
ROCKET'S SOUND ?

THEY SEEM TO BE THE SKULLS OF ALL THOSE PEOPLE WHO CAME HUNTING FOR THE TREASURE, GOT KILLED AND NEVER RETURNED.

TODAY TWO MORE SKULLS
WILL BE ADDED IN THE
PILE

HIT !!
KILL !

LET'S SEE, WHOSE
SKULL GETS
ADDED IN
THE
PILE.

SABU ! DON'T LET GO.

HU-HUBA !
?!!

THUD !

AA-AA-AA !

CHACHAJI ! LET'S ENTER THE ROOM WHICH HAS THE TREASURE.

WHAT IS THE APPROXIMATE VALUE OF THIS TREASURE ?
THEY ARE INVALUABLE. THEY MIGHT BE WORTH MILLIONS OF RUPEES.

GR GR
GRGRRRR !
?

CRACKKKKK !
SABU ! EARTHQUAKE...! RUN !!

OHHH !

MOVE UPWARDS FROM THIS DARK WELL.
THANK GOD WE CAN BREATHE FRESH AIR.
CHACHAJI ! DO YOU KNOW WHAT'S IN MY HAND?
WHAT ?
DIAMOND ! YOU GOT ONE FROM THE TREASURE.
JEWELLERS
THIS DIAMOND IS WORTH MORE THAN 50 CRORES !
CHACHAJI ! HE FAINTED ON HEARING THIS.

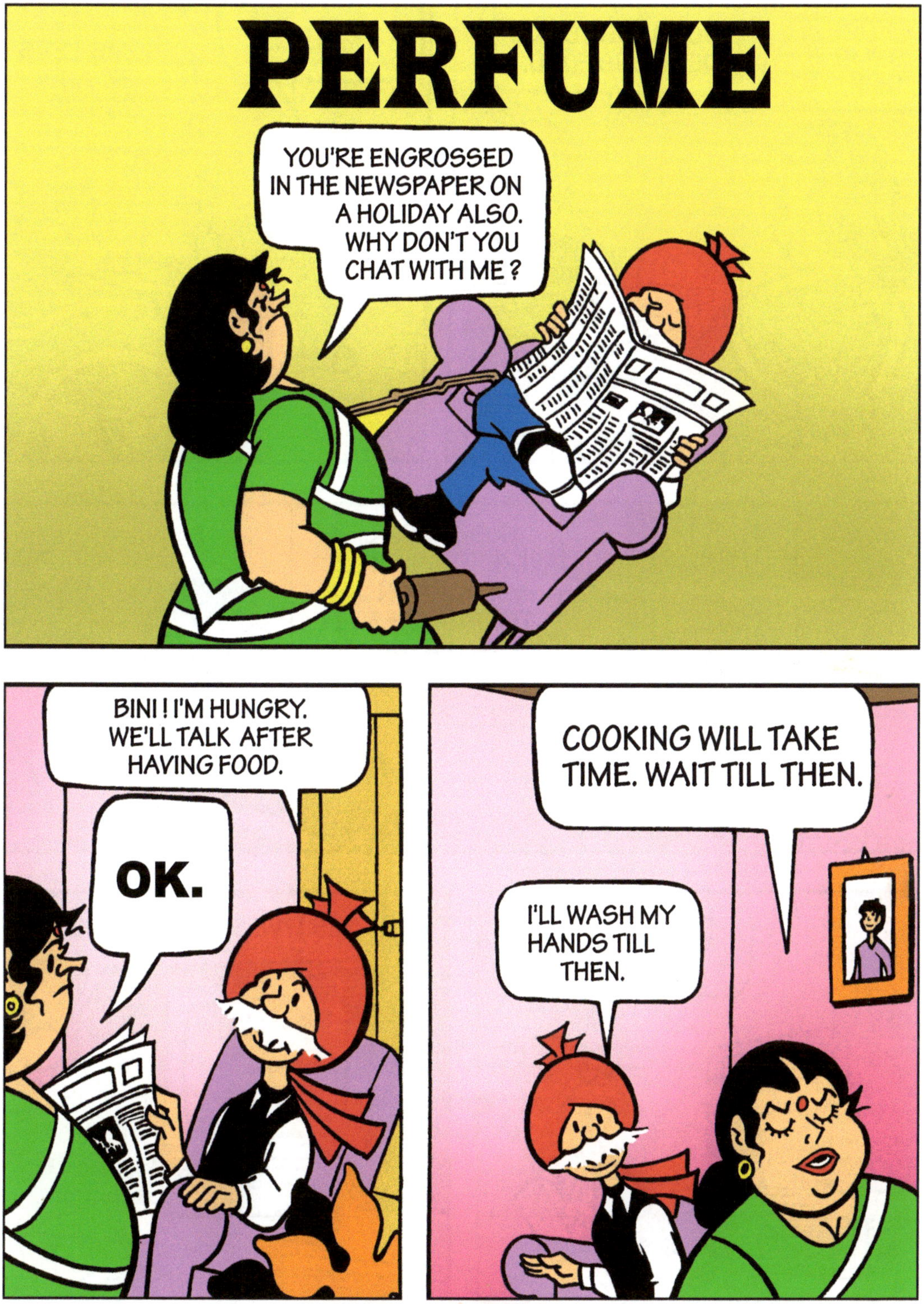

PERFUME

YOU'RE ENGROSSED IN THE NEWSPAPER ON A HOLIDAY ALSO. WHY DON'T YOU CHAT WITH ME ?

AFTER SOME TIME....
WOW ! YOU COOK DELICIOUS FOOD.

I'M FULL.
COME, LET'S SIT AND GOSSIP.

I REMEMBER. I'VE TO FINISH MY WORK ON THE INTERNET.

HAVE TO SEND AN IMPORTANT E-MAIL.

YES ! I'VE SENT THE MAIL.
BONO
ADDRESS

I'M JUST A SERVANT IN THIS HOUSE.

I'M GOING TO MY MOM'S PLACE.

LEERA! WHAT'S IN YOUR HAND?
STORE

IT'S A PERFUME TO ATTRACT THE MENFOLK.
GIVE IT TO ME. I REQUIRE IT.

AHA!! WONDERFUL FRAGRANCE.

I'LL USE THE ENTIRE BOTTLE. HUBBY DEAR WOULD BE MESMERIZED.

WOW ! WHAT A FASCINATING FRAGRANCE.

YOUR FRAGRANCE IS ATTRACTING ME.

THIS PERFUME... I CAN'T CONTROL MYSELF.

LEERA'S PERFUME IS VERY EFFECTIVE.

THE PERFUME IS HAVING AN IMPACT ON HIM ALSO.
www.chachachaudhary.com

SNEEEEEZE !!!

WHAT HAPPENED?
SNEEEEEZE !!!
DON'T YOU KNOW THAT ?---

I'M ALLERGIC TO PERFUMES?
SNEEEEEZE !!!
I HAVE THE REMEDY....

WEATHER

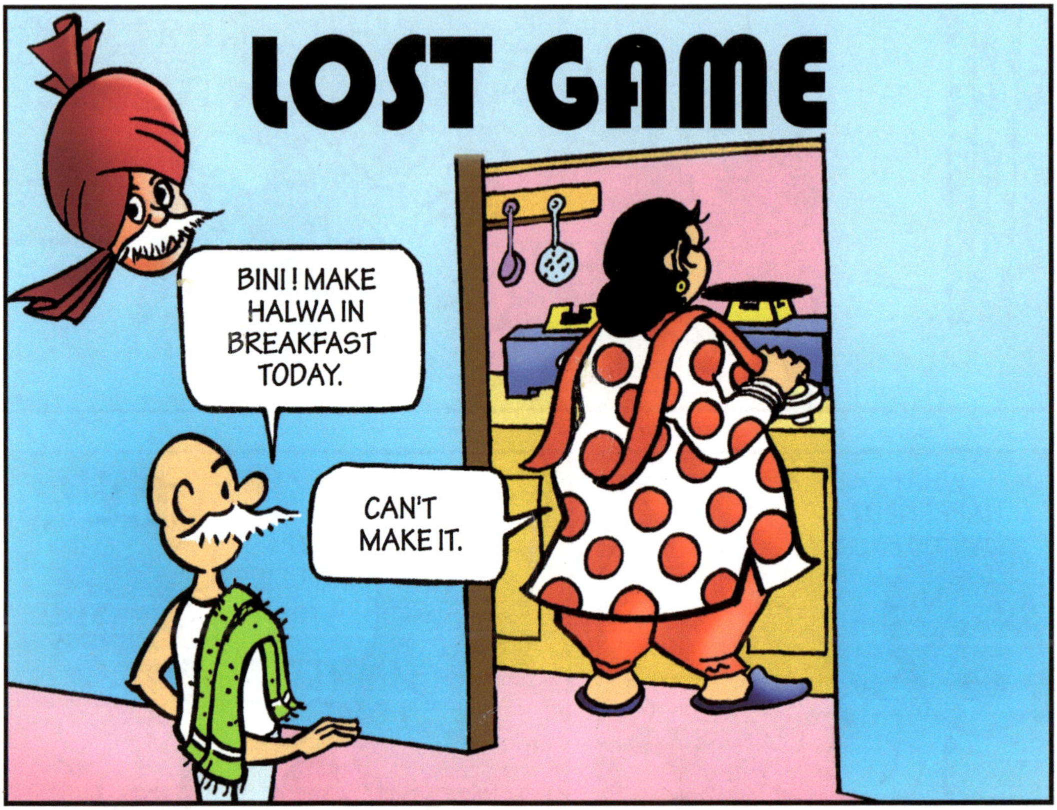

LOST GAME

BINI ! MAKE HALWA IN BREAKFAST TODAY.

CAN'T MAKE IT.

I'LL GET GHEE AT THAT STORE.

GHEE
THE CANISTER IS HEAVY.

GHEE
DALDO ! WE HAVE TO STEAL THE GHEE CANISTER.
OK.

GHEE
CHACHAJI ! YOU MUST BE TIRED. TAKE SOME REST AT MY PLACE.

GHEE
COME, LET'S HAVE A CUP OF HOT TEA.

LEAVE THE CANISTER OUTSIDE. THERE'S NO RISK HERE.

JUST WAIT FOR 5 MINUTES.

SPECIAL CARDAMOM TEA IS READY.

CHAUDHARY IS BUSY IN HAVING TEA. I'LL ESCAPE WITH THIS TIN.

BARK ! BARK !!

HU-HU-HU !
YOU'RE MISTAKEN.
THERE'S SOME TROUBLE OUTSIDE. MY DOG IS ALARMING ME.

SO, YOU'RE ESCAPING WITH MY GHEE ?
BARK !!

NO ! YOU WERE TIRED SO MY HUSBAND WANTED TO HELP YOU.

YES ! I PICKED UP THE TIN TO HELP YOU IN DROPPING IT HOME.
GHEE

THEN, FOLLOW ME.

HURRY UP, I'M HUNGRY.
www.chachachaudhary.com

BINI, I'VE BROUGHT THE GHEE.

THANKS FOR THE HELP. WE'LL MEET AGAIN.
GHEE

HE GOT A FREE CUP OF TEA.
AND I HAD TO BE A PORTER ALSO.

IT WAS A LOST GAME.

HEAVY PURSE

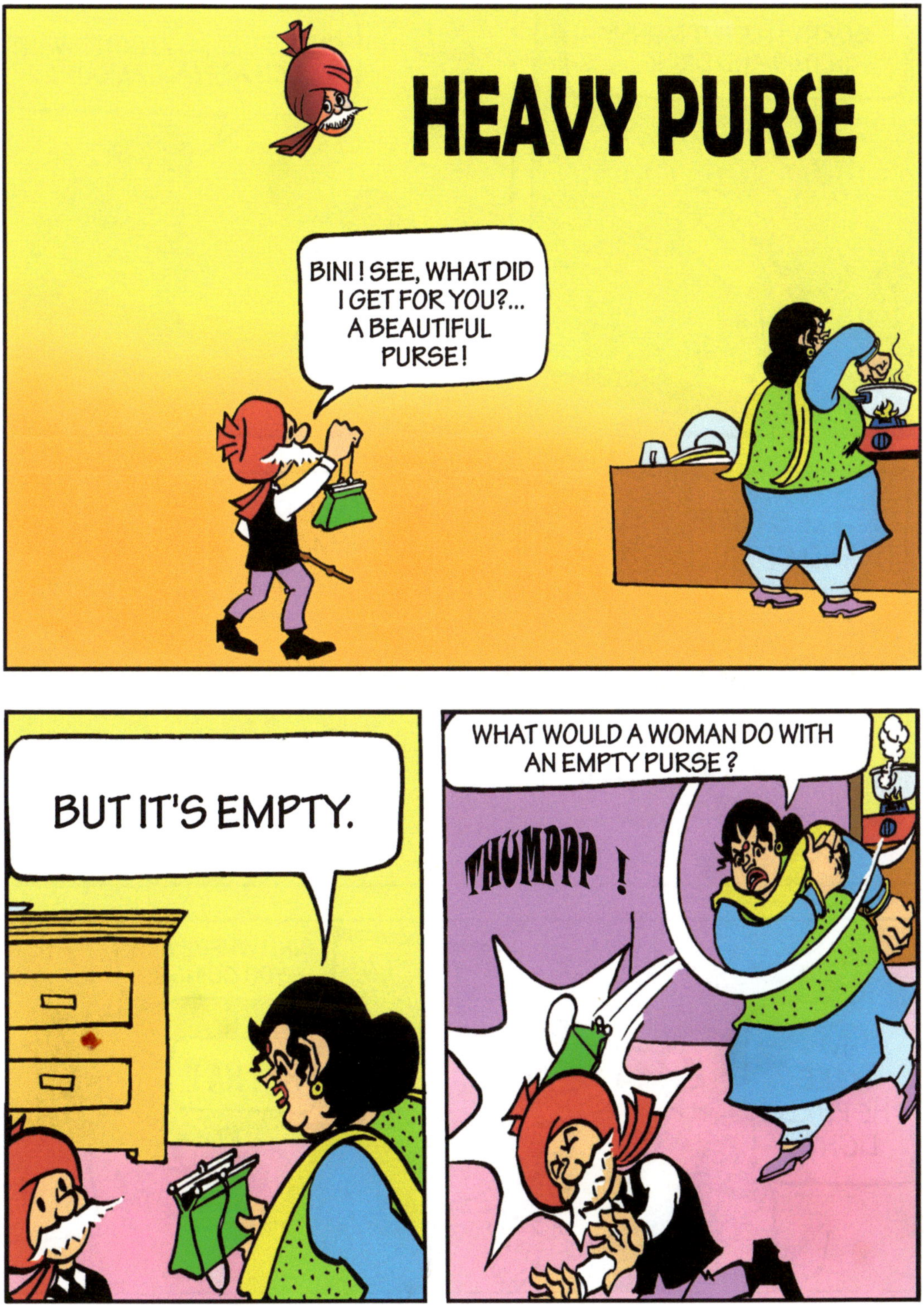

BINI ! SEE, WHAT DID I GET FOR YOU?... A BEAUTIFUL PURSE !

SORRY ! I'LL PUT MONEY IN THIS AND BRING.

ONLY 5 BUCKS ? I DON'T WANT SUCH A SMALL AMOUNT.

OK ! I'LL STUFF IT AND COME.

TAKE ! I'VE MADE IT HEAVY.

BINI ! WHERE ARE YOU GOING ?
TO MAKE THE PURSE LIGHT.
HA ! HA !!

GIVE SOMETHING TO THE POOR BEGGAR.

I DON'T OPEN THE PURSE IN PUBLIC TO GIVE ALMS.

THAN WHAT SHOULD I DO ? OPEN A DEPARTMENTAL STORE TO BEG... ?
DLF.

DHOL! WHY DON'T WE ESCAPE AWAY WITH THAT FATSO'S ENTIRE PURSE ?
BUT RODA, HER GRIP IS VERY TIGHT.

I'LL SPREAD SHAMPOO AROUND. WHEN SHE'LL SLIP, THE PURSE WILL FALL AWAY.

SLIPPP!
OUCHHHHH!

THUD!

RODA! HOW DID THIS EGG SHAPED SWELLING COME ON YOUR HEAD?
MY PURSE!

BECAUSE I STUFFED IT WITH ONE RUPEE COINS.

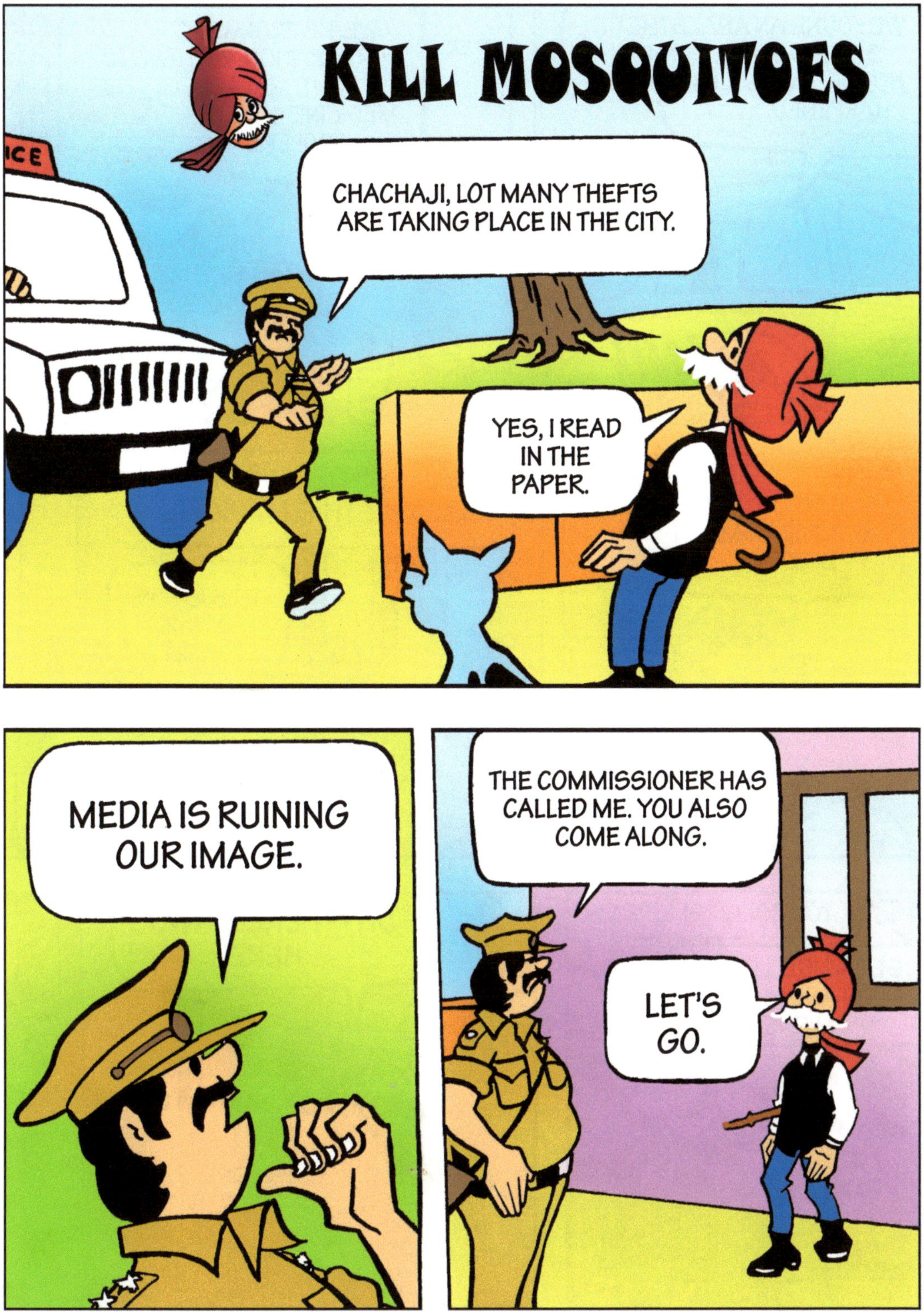

KILL MOSQUITOES

ICE

CHACHAJI, LOT MANY THEFTS ARE TAKING PLACE IN THE CITY.

YES, I READ IN THE PAPER.

WE FOUND AN ANAESTHETIC SPREAD IN ALL THOSE HOUSES WHERE THE THEFT HAPPENED.

AFTER 2 HOURS..
WE 'RE FROM CITY CORPORATION. WE HAVE TO PUT ANTI MALARIA MEDICINE IN ALL THE COOLERS.

MY HUSBAND ISN'T AT HOME. COME LATER.

MOSQUITOES WILL BE KILLED BY THIS MEDICINE
THIS IS FOR YOUR SAFETY.

YOU COME TOMORROW.
GET ASIDE. LET ME GO IN AND PUT THE MEDICINE.

OH ! THERE'S A DOG HERE.
WOOF-WOOF !!

STOP THIS DOG ! SO THAT WE CAN DO OUR WORK.
ROCKET DOESN'T ALLOW STRANGERS INSIDE.
BOW ! WOW !

MOSQUITO BITE WILL GIVE YOU DENGUE ! YOU'LL DIE.

ROGAN ! NOW WE HAVE TO GO TO B BLOCK.

BINI ! I'VE COME.

WE'RE ABOUT TO DIE OF MALARIA AND DENGUE.
WHY SO ?

CORPORATION PEOPLE HAD COME TO PUT MEDICINE. THEY LEFT DUE TO ROCKET'S BARKING.

ROCKET BARKS ONLY WHEN HE SENSES ANY DANGER. WHERE DID THEY GO ?

TOWARDS B BLOCK.

WE'VE TO GO THERE.

WAIT. YOUR MEDICINE NEEDS TO BE CHECKED.

ROGAN ! RUN !
WAIT !

OHH !
YOU'VE BEEN TOLD TO WAIT.
MOSQUITOES ARE HOVERING AROUND.
THEY USED TO PUT INTOXICATING MEDICINE IN THE COOLER TO MAKE EVERYONE UNCONSCIOUS. THEN THEIR GANG STEALS AND RUNS AWAY.
LEAVE TOPAN.

POLICE
OH ! POLICE !

WHAT'S THE MATTER HERE?

INSPECTOR MOZA ! WE CAUGHT 2 MOSQUITOES.

REST WILL BE COUGHT BY US.
POLICE

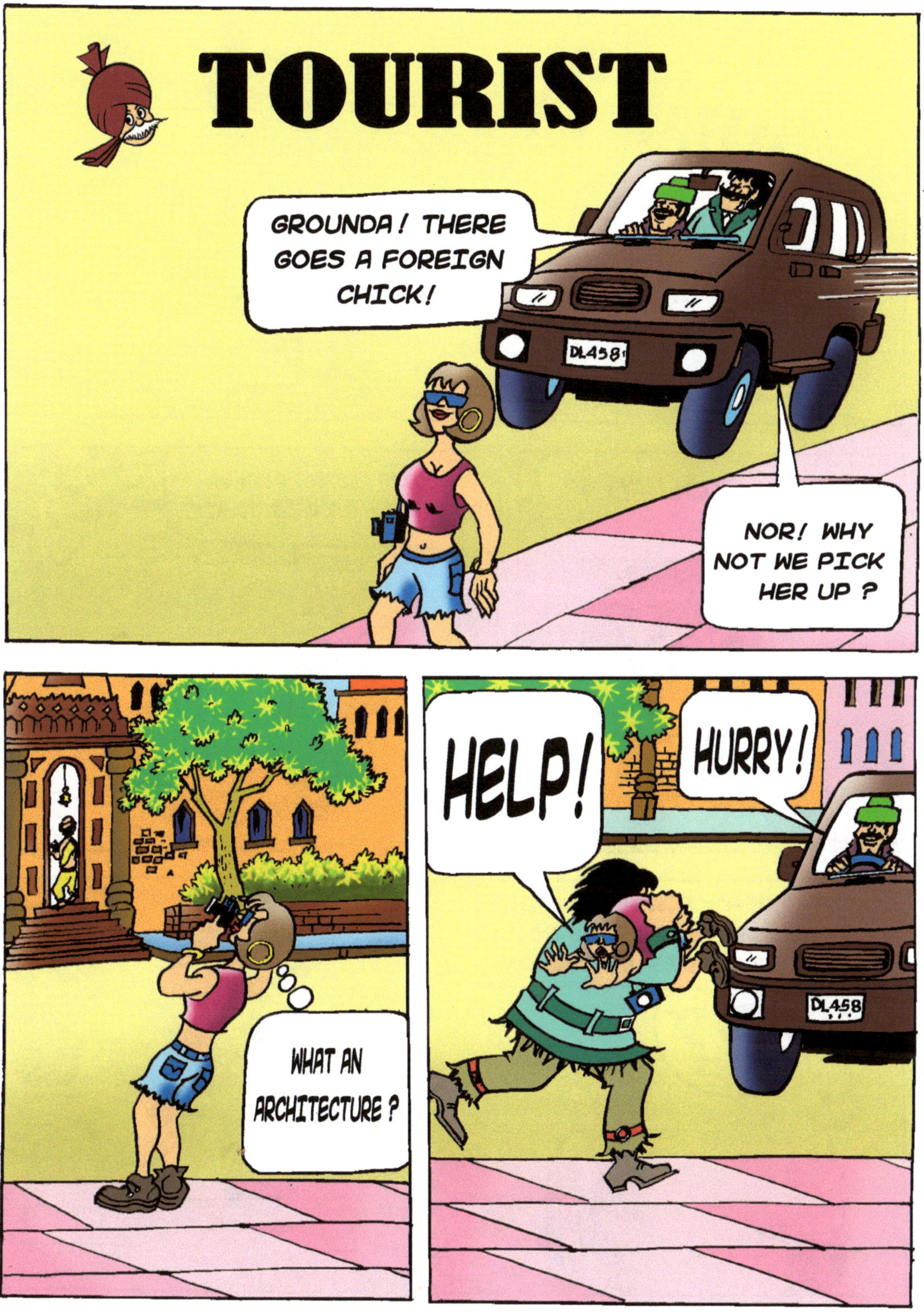

TOURIST

GROUNDA! THERE GOES A FOREIGN CHICK!

NOR! WHY NOT WE PICK HER UP ?

THUMP P!
AUOOWW!

RAT! -- YOU HIT ME ?

WE MUST RESPECT A WOMAN, PARTICULARLY A FOREIGN TOURIST!

GET READY FOR PUNISHMENT! GROUNDA'S EARS ARE NOT HABITUAL TO LISTEN SERMONS!
?!

WHAMM!

RED TURBAN! THERE IS STILL MY LEFT HAND!

FIRST, TAKE IT!
THUDD!
OOWCHH!

OOHH!

NAMASTE! -- AND THANK YOU! WHAT THEY CALL YOU ?
CHACHA CHAUDHARY! OR UNCLE CHAUDHARY!

DON'T YOU KNOW, A LION DOES NOT LET HIS PREY GO ?

WHISTLE !

JUMP

JUMP!
BOOMM!
AAWW!

TAKE THIS!
BANG
G!

WHAMM!
I DON'T LIKE VIOLENCE! BUT SOME PERSONS COMPEL ME!

BETTER TO RUN BEFORE WE GET THRASHING!
SHOES
DL 45 81

CHACHA CHAUDHARY™

BIG HEAD

A TRAIL OF TRUCKS IS STOPPED AT OUTSKIRT OF THE CITY.

CHECKING !

SIR, WATERMELONS ! IF YOU WANT, TAKE TWO-THREE FOR YOUR CHILDREN .

YOU CAN GO .

HOLD ON!
I WANT TO HAVE
A GLANCE!

LET HIM GO, CHACHA CHAUDHARY!
WHY TO WASTE TIME ?
RAHIM! WHAT'S
HARM IN LOOKING
AGAIN ?

PULL DOWN THE COVER!
I HAVE NEVER SEEN A
COVER LIKE QUILT!
I SMELL A RAT!

CHACHA CHAUDHARY'S
BRAIN WORKS FASTER
THAN A COMPUTER.
LOOK! PACKETS OF
CONTRABAND DRUGS
STOP THE
TRUCK!

RUN !
GRRR!

WHAM M !
BOOM!BOOM !!
CHASE THEM!

SABU!
A SMUGGLERS'
TRUCK GOES!
STOP
THAT!

ESCAPED!
GULLU ! PRESS
ACCELERATOR!
COPS MAY
CHASE!

THEY ARE NOWHERE!
WE'VE GONE THROUGH
MANY SUCH HURDLES!

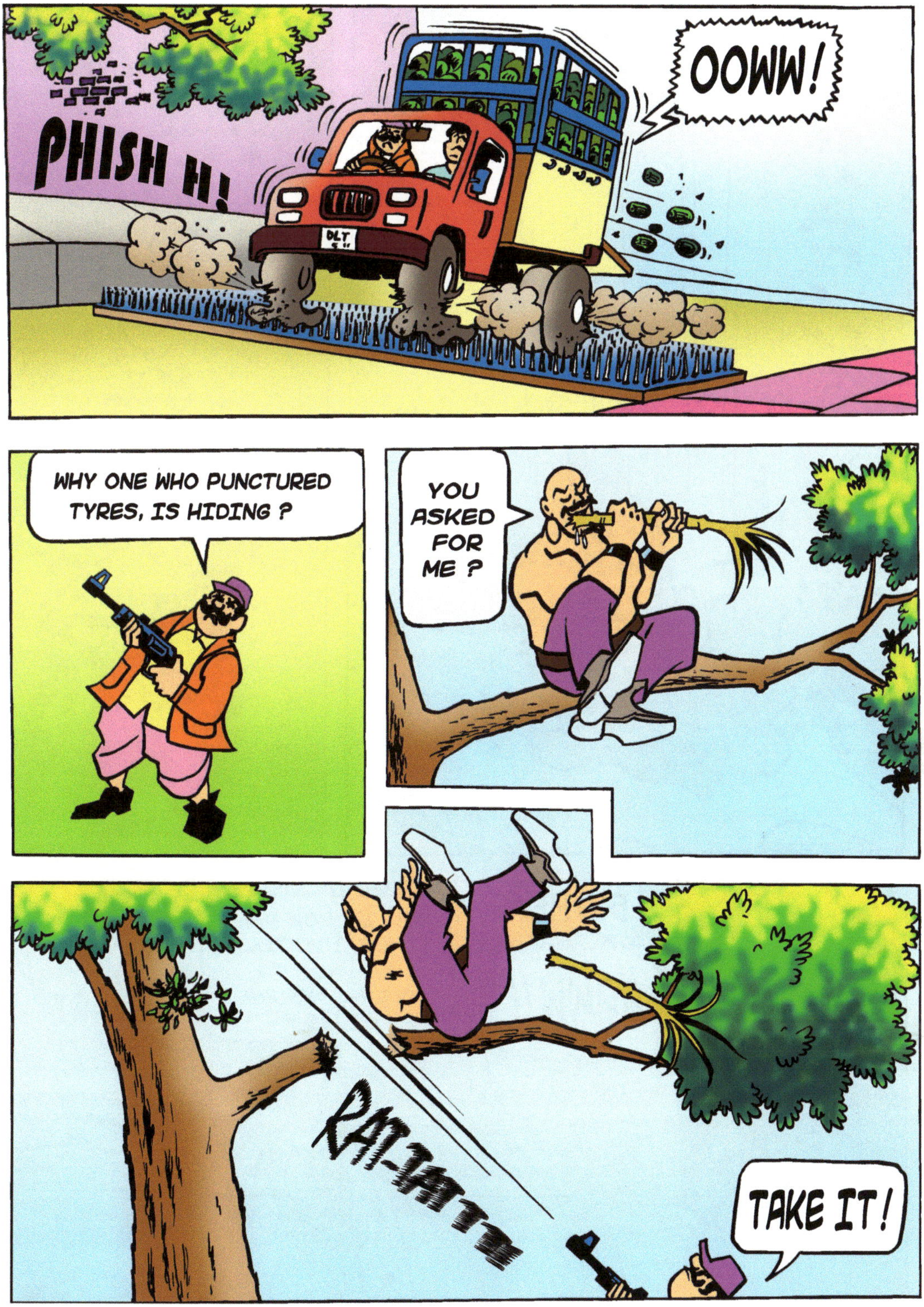

WHY ONE WHO PUNCTURED TYRES, IS HIDING ?

YOU ASKED FOR ME ?

TAKE IT!

CRACK!!

MY BACK!

OOHH!

BIG HEAD.
AAWW!!
GULLU ! HOW MANY TIMES, I'VE TOLD YOU NOT TO OVER-CONSUME DRUGS ?

SIR! IT'S SABU, WHO DID THIS TO HIM!
WHO'S HE ?

SIR! HE IS A MUSCULAR STRONG MAN!

WHO MAY HE BE, BUT WE CAN'T ABANDON DRUGS WORTH CRORES! CHANGE CLOTHES! WE HAVE TO GO!

START ENGINE!

HOPE, THEY MUST BE THERE!

ONCE COMMODITIES ARE IN POLICE CUSTODY, IT'S DIFFICULT TO RETRIEVE THOSE!

GIVE OUR GOODS BACK!
BUT THOSE ARE CONTRABAND!

RAT-TATT!
I HATE CHATTER BUGS!

NOW NO HURDLE!

PUMPKIN HEAD! HAVEN'T HEARD THAT DRUGS HAVE BEEN CONFISCATED?
IF YOU DARE TO TOUCH THESE DRUGS, YOU ALL WILL BE SMASHED.

KILL!
RAT-TAT-TT!

TICK! TICK!
TICK!! TICK!!
YOUR GAME IS OVER!

WHAM !!!
MY REAL STRENGTH IS MY HEAD!

SABU! IF YOU CONTROL SKY, GROUND'LL AUTOMATICALLY BE CONQUERED!

HU-HUBA!

WHEN SABU IS ANGRY, A VOLCANO ERUPTS SOMEWHERE!

PROUD OF HEAD ? WHY NOT I DEFLATE IT ?
OH, LEAVE ME!

SWOOSH H !
GO!

GULLU! RUN !!

WHERE TO ? GIVE US A CHANCE TO SERVE YOU FOR FEW DAYS!
?!

WHERE WERE YOU WANDERING PICKING QUARRELS ? EVER THOUGHT OF MEALS ?

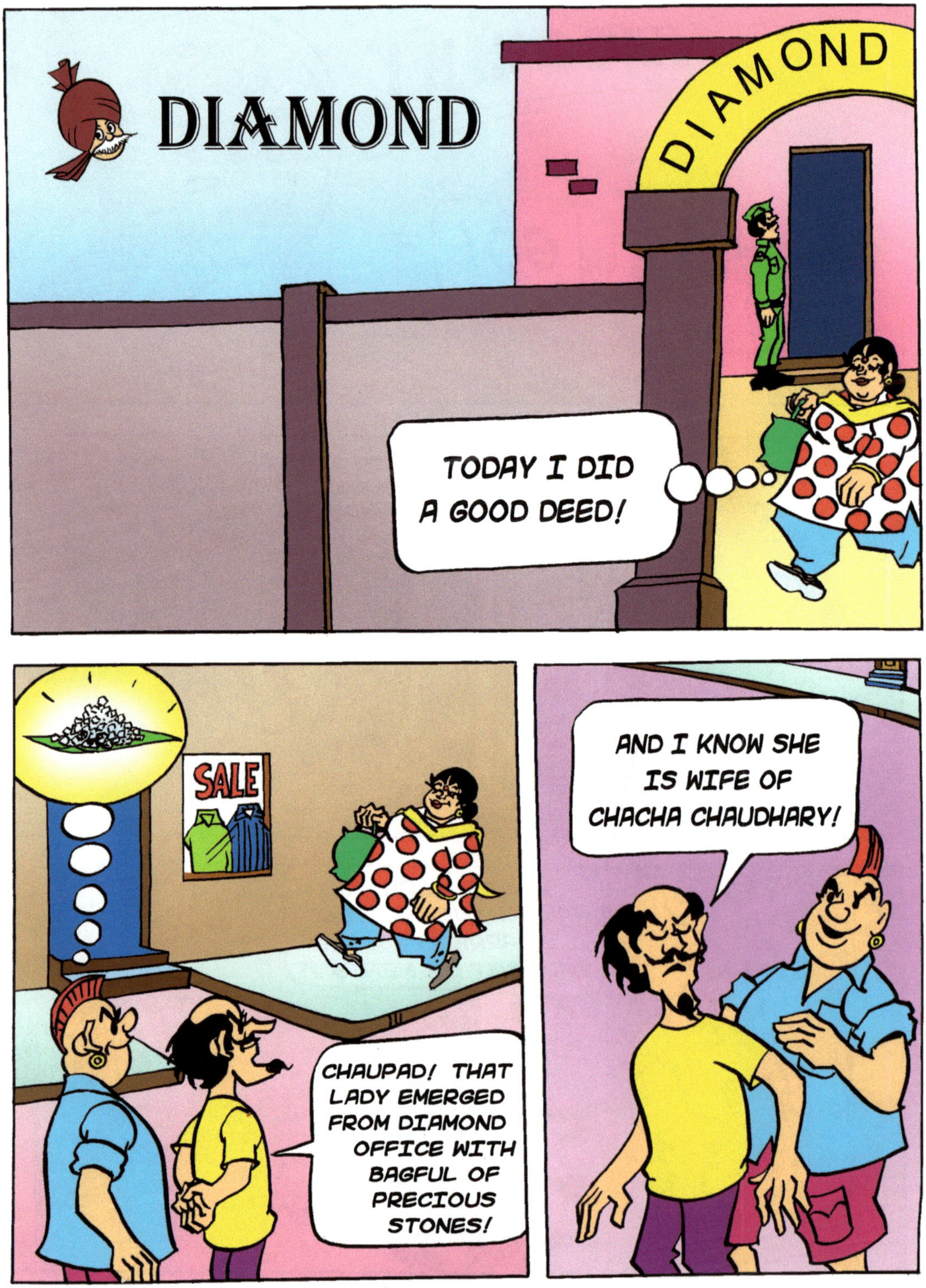

DIAMOND

DIAMOND

TODAY I DID A GOOD DEED!

RAUPAD! WHOEVER SHE MAY BE, OUR CONCERN IS HER BAG!

BUT HOW WOULD WE WHISK HER DIAMONDS ?
FOR THAT WE HAVE TO POSE ONE OF US AS A TV REPORTER!
airtel

STOP HER , WHILE I'LL FETCH A CAMERA!

?
MADAM WAIT!

MY COLLEAGUE WANTS TO INTERVIEW YOU FOR A TV CHANNEL!
MINE?

YOU'RE MISTAKEN! I AM NEITHER A MINISTER NOR A FILM STAR!

WHAT COULD BE MORE THAN BEING WIFE OF CHACHA CHAUDHARY?

THERE REPORTER HAS ARRIVED!
OKAY! --- LET ME DO SOME MAKE UP!
TRAVEL
VISIT

THERE IS BENEFIT OF BEING FAT! I CAN LIFT HEAVY WEIGHT AND ROGUES LOSE THEIR CONSCIOUS WITH MY RIGHT HAND HIT!

MY BAG ?

RUN! FATTY IS CHASING!
I CAN'T WITH HEAVY CAMERA!

RAUPUD! LEAVE CAMERA! WE CAN BUY MORE WITH ONE DIAMOND!

OKAY!
THUMPP!

BINI! WHAT IS THE SCENE?

TWO ROGUES LEFT THIS CAMERA! DEAR, MAY I SHOOT YOUR MOVIE?

MADAM! TAKE YOUR BAG AND RETURN OUR CAMERA!

WHEN WE OPENED IT, THERE WERE GLASS PEBBLES INSIDE! WE THOUGHT BAG MIGHT CONTAIN DIAMONDS!

COME! LET ME SHOW YOU THE SECRET!

SCHOOL IS CELEBRATING DIAMOND JUBILEE! THE PRINCIPAL GAVE ME GLASS PEBBLES TO HOLD A STALL OF GAMES!
DIAMOND JUBILEE

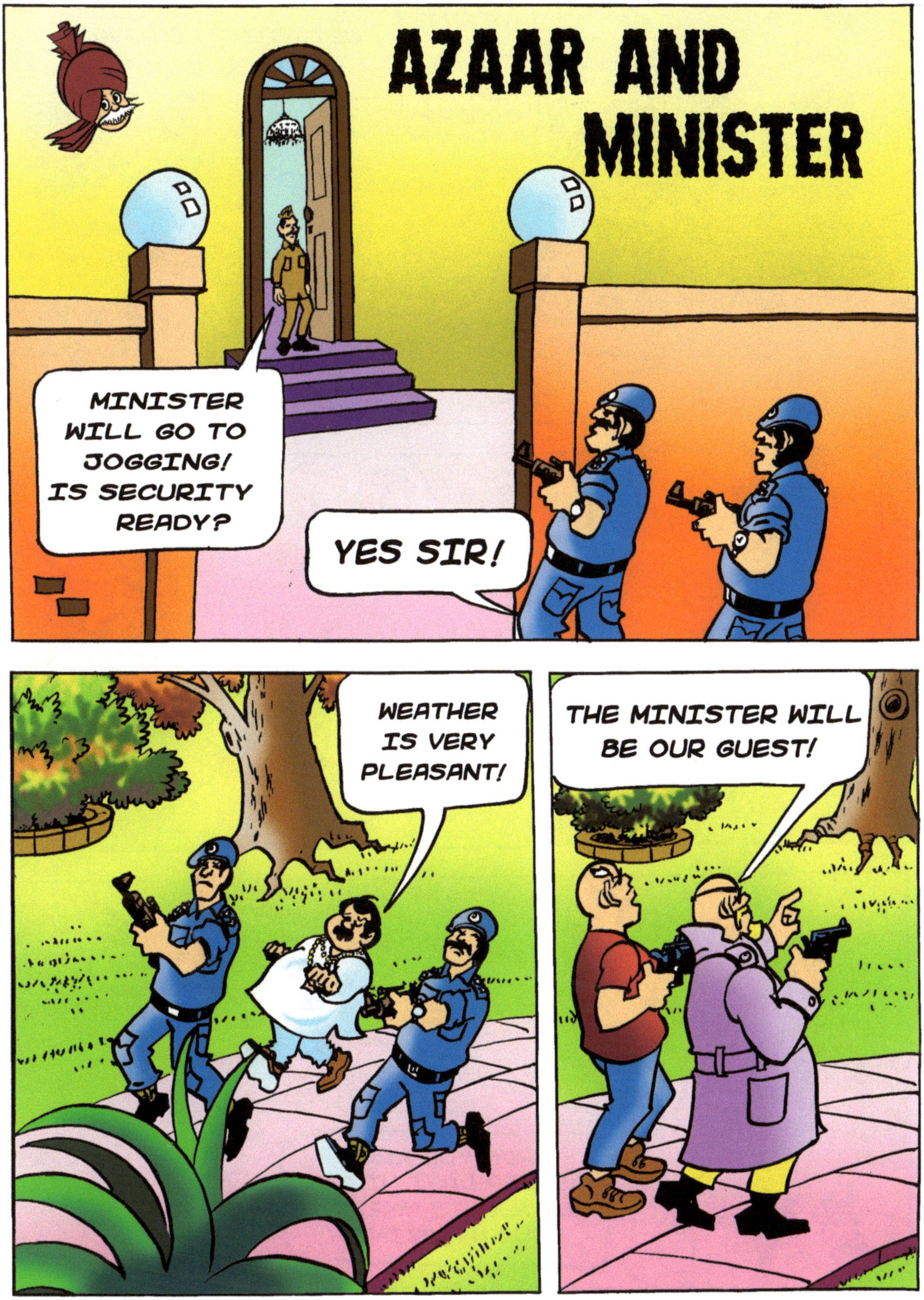

AZAAR AND MINISTER

DIDN'T YOU HEAR AZAAR'S ORDER?
GET ASIDE! WE HAVE ORDER TO SHOOT!

OKAY! YOU FIRE FIRST!

??
?!
TICK!
TICKK!

RAT-TAT TT!
AAWW!
WHEN YOU WERE ASLEEP LAST NIGHT, OUR AGENTS EMPTIED YOUR MAGAZINES!

WHERE ARE YOU TAKING ME TO ?

SIR! YOU EARNED THOUSAND OF CRORES IN SCAMS! WE'LL SET YOU FREE WHEN WE GET OUR SHARE!

CHACHA CHAUDHARY! THE MINISTER IS MADE HOSTAGE! KIDNAPPERS THREATENED TO KILL HIM IF RANSOM IS NOT PAID IN A DAY!

THE WICKED MINISTER IS A KNOWN CORRUPT!
CHACHAJI! IT'S FOR THE COURT TO PUT HIM ON TRIAL, NOT WE!

SABU, WHAT DO YOU SAY ?
TOSS THE BALL! IF ROCKET CATCHES THAT, WE'LL GO! OTHERWISE NOT!

BALL TOSS!

THUMP!

MOBILES
WE'LL HAVE TO REACH THE SPOT OF INCIDENT TO FIND ANY CLUE!
Shoes
BANK
ATM
LOANS
000

FOUND A PEARL WHICH THE MINISTER WORE IN CHAIN!
000

MORE PEARLS! PERHAPS THE HOSTAGE'S CHAIN BROKE DURING SCUFFLE!

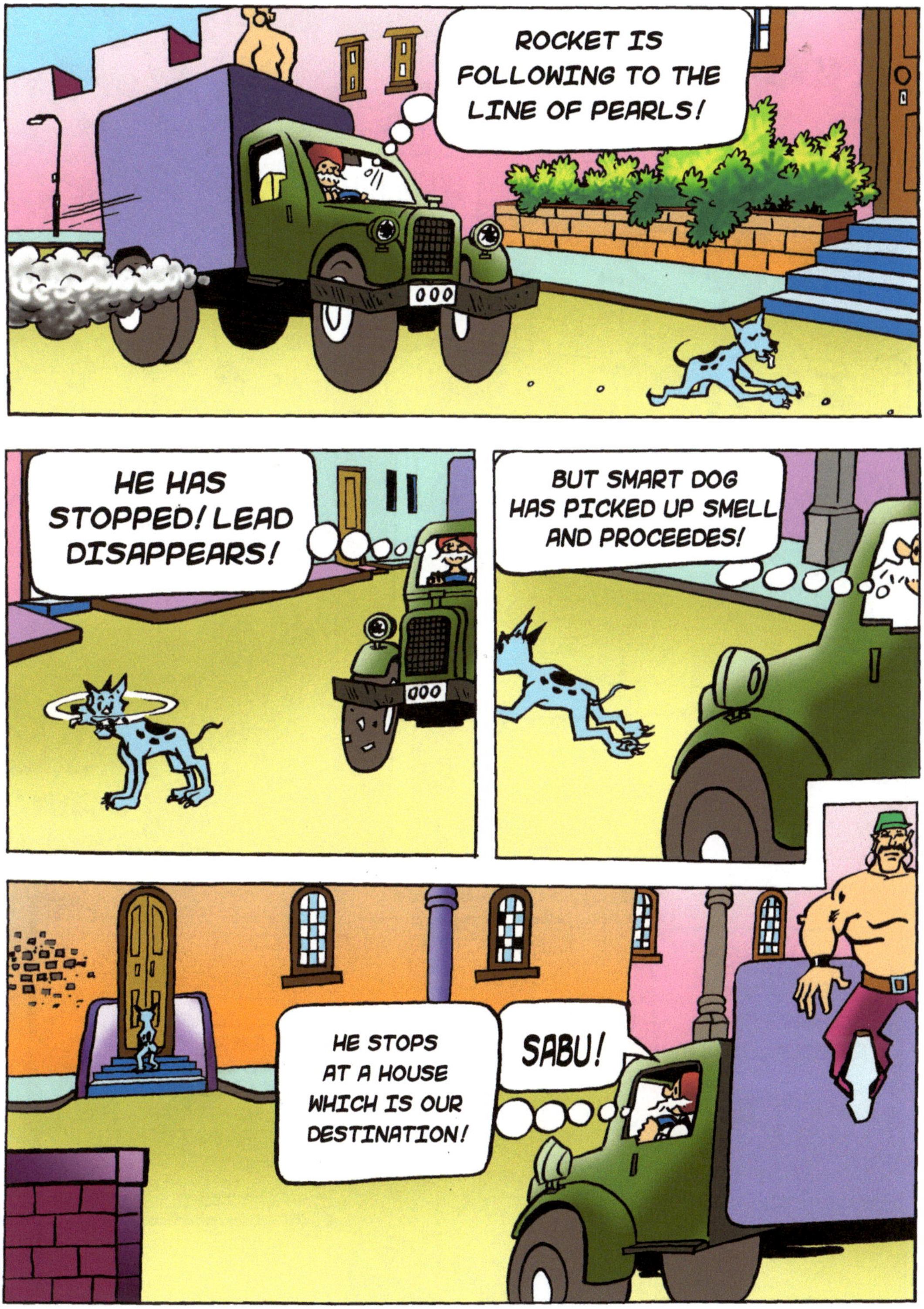

HE HAS STOPPED! LEAD DISAPPEARS!

BUT SMART DOG HAS PICKED UP SMELL AND PROCEEDES!

HE STOPS AT A HOUSE WHICH IS OUR DESTINATION!

SABU!

KARRRBOOM!
HU-HUBA!

KILL!
KARRRBOOM!

WHAM M!
OOWW!

MINISTER SAHAB! A COMMON MAN RESCUED YOU!
I REPENT! I PROMISE TO RETURN THE ILLGOTTEN MONEY TO PUBLIC!
000

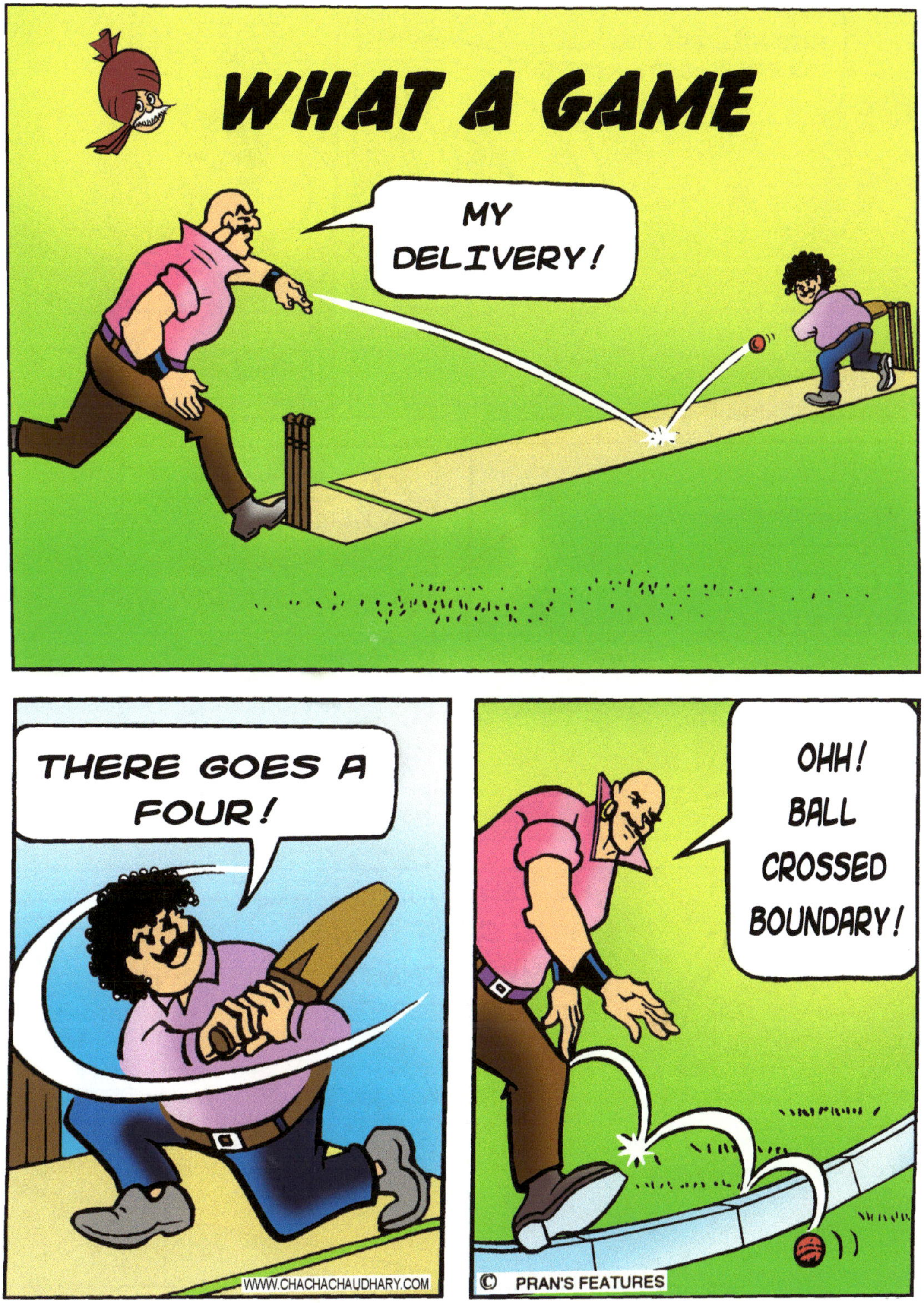

WHAT A GAME

MY DELIVERY!

THIS WILL GET YOU CLEAN BOWLED !

IT IS GOING TO BE A SIX!

OH! IT IS TOO HIGH!

A SIX!

YOU CAN'T TAKE MY WICKET!

I AM GETTING TIRED!

SWOOSH H !

WHAM M !

OHH! AGAIN FOUR!

CHACHAJI! I AM UNABLE TO GET THE WICKET OF KAMAAL!

HE'S A THIRD RATE BATSMAN!

HE HITS WITH HIS NEW BAT!
WELL!

MR. KAMAAL! I AM YOUR FAN!
THANKS!

COULD WE SHAKE HANDS?
WHY NOT?

CHAUDHARY! NOW ENJOY MY BATTING!

SABU! DELIVER THE NEXT BALL!

SWOOSH!

I'LL SEND THIS TOO TO BOUNDARY!

OWW! I SLIPPED BAT!

MY BAT?
Kaddaaak

LOOK! THE BAT IS FITTED WITH HIDDEN SPRINGS!

THAT WERE THOSE SPRINGS WHICH GAVE PUSH TO HIT FOURS AND SIXES!

HA! HA!! WHAT A CRICKET!

HONEY
AND
DAHIPAL

SABU! WHAT MADE YOU STOP?
CHACHAJI! YOU GO HOME!

I'LL TAKE REST IN THE COOL BREEZE!

WELL, AS YOU WISH!
© PRAN'S FEATURES

DAHIPAL! I AM COMING ACROSS THE RIVER TO MEET YOU!
NO, HONEY! YOU'LL DROWN!
WWW.CHACHACHAUDHARY.COM

INSTEAD, I'LL SWIM ACROSS !

I WILL GET GOOD SLEEP IN THE FRESH AIR!

WHY IS MY NATTU CRYING ?
BAPU ! I LOVE HONEY, BUT SHE LOVES DAHIPAL !-- I WANT HONEY !

OHH !

HELP ! HELP !!

HELP ! HELP !!
THE BOY IS IN DANGER, SABU !

SPLASH H !

ONE SHOULD NOT GET SO MAD IN LOVE TO JUMP IN RIVER !

THERE ARE FOOTPRINTS OF SOMEONE ALSO ! THAT INDICATES THE BOY WAS PUSHED INTO WATER !

STRANGER'S FOOTPRINTS LEAD TO THE VEHICLE ON ROAD !

NOKIA
50% SALE
TOOLS
WE HAVE TO FOLLOW THAT CAR !

OPTICIAN
FLATS
OBILE
BANK
TYRE
Confectionary
CAR LOAN
SALE
ARFES
SABU ! WE ARE NEAR OUR DESTINATION !

BAJARANGI HIRED DHAMAKASINGH TO KILL DAHIPAL, BECAUSE HIS SON LOVED HONEY, WHO LIKED DAHIPAL !
CHACHA CHAUDHARY'S BRAIN WORKS FASTER THAN A COMPUTER.

YOU CAN'T LEAVE ALIVE !
RAT-TAT-TT!
SABU'S MUSCLES ARE OF JUPITER ! BULLETS DON'T EFFECT THEM !

WHAM M!
COCKROACH, GO !

POLICE STATION
WHERE AM I ?
AT THE RIGHT PLACE !

INSPECTOR MOZA ! ARREST BAJARANGI !
WHAT DID I DO? DHAMAKA SINGH PUSHED DAHIPAL INTO RIVER !

ONE WHO CONSPIRES IS EQUALLY GUILTY !

THANKS, CHACHAJI !
DAHIPAL ! DON'T FORGET TO INVITE US ON YOUR WEDDING !

BOGO-GOGO

ROBBERS ! THEY HAVE WHISKED MY CAR !

WE LEFT HIM FAR BEHIND !

BOGO ! WE HAVE A CAR ! WHAT ABOUT THE PETROL EXPENSES ?
GOGO ! WE'LL MANAGE THAT!

CAN'T FIND A TAXI ! HOW WILL I REACH THE AIRPORT ?

HE'S WAITING FOR TAXI !

WHERE DO YOU WANT TO GO, SIR ?
AIRPORT !

TAXI WOULD CHARGE YOU Rs. 1000/- IF YOU PAY Rs. 500/- IN ADVANCE, WE'LL DROP YOU THERE !

HERE IS A Rs. 500/- NOTE !

HERE WE GO ! WE HAVE TO BUY PETROL !
HEY !-- MY MONEY !

HO ! HO !! TO THE PETROL PUMP !
NOKIA

CHACHA JI ! TWO ROBBERS TOOK MY MONEY AND WENT TO THE PETROL PUMP ! I HAD TO REACH THE AIRPORT !

LET'S FIRST SEND YOU TO THE AIRPORT !--- ONE--TWO—

AND THREE !

AIRPORT
CHACHA CHAUDHARY IS GREAT !
THUMP!

COME SABU, THIS IS A SHORT CUT TO THE PETROL PUMP !

FILL PETROL WORTH Rs. 500/-

STOLEN CAR AND FREE PETROL ?
GOGO RUN !

SABU !
CRUSH HIM !

WHAMM !
SWOOSH H H !

OHH ! WHAT HAVE YOU DONE TO MY CAR ?

THEY'LL PAY FOR THE REPAIRS !

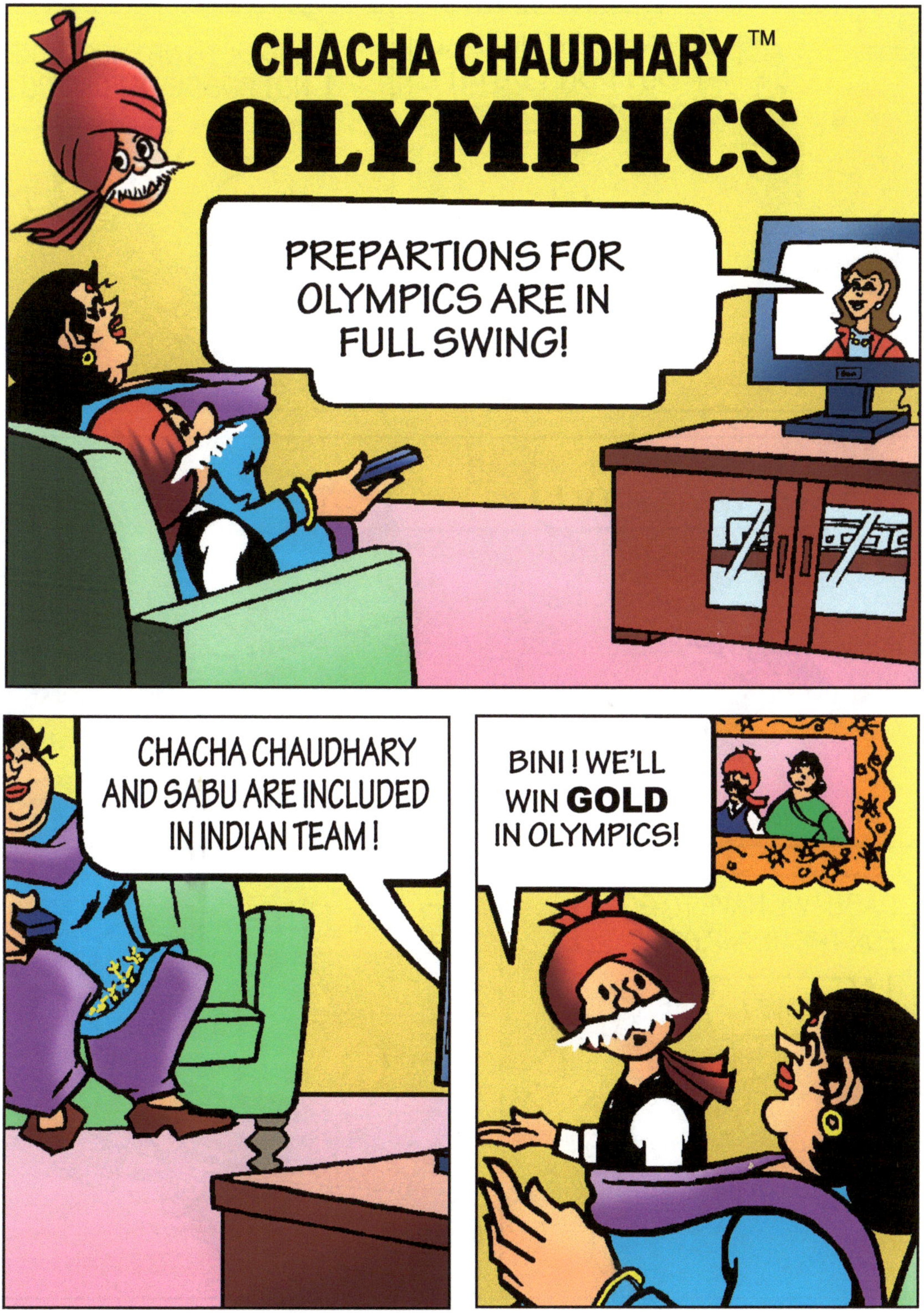

CHACHA CHAUDHARY™
OLYMPICS

PREPARTIONS FOR OLYMPICS ARE IN FULL SWING!

WIN A GOLD MEDAL !
BUT DON'T BUY IT !

AND BOTH OF THESE ARE
NOT POSSIBLE FOR YOU !

HERE I GO !
YOU WATCH TV !

SABU ! WE HAVE TO GO
FOR THE OLYMPICS !
WOW !

THEY FLY–
WWW.CHACHACHAUDHARY.COM

ARCHERY

OHH !
I MISSED
TARGET !

CHACHAJI ! YOUR TURN !
I'LL PLAY IN MY OWN STYLE !

CHACHA CHAUDHARY BLINDFOLDS HIMSELF--

SWOOSH H H!..
WOW !
WAHH !

HE HAS MADE A RECORD !

SHOTPUT

SWISH H!

WOW, PREVIOUS RECORD BEATEN !

NEXT COMPETITOR
SABU !
BRAVO !

SWOOSH H H

WHERE HAS THE BALL GONE ?
INTO THE SPACE !

YOUR RECORD WILL NEVER BE BEATEN !

CHACHA CHAUDHARY & SABU BOTH HAVE WON **GOLD MEDALS !**
HURRAY !

Help the pencils to get to the middle of the maze and color the butterfly and flowers.

Match the pictures to their shadows.